The Mystery

"What's all the mystery?" I asked.

"That's just it," Stephanie replied. "I don't know. I thought my parents were going to tell me at dinner. . . ."

Katie, Patti, and I waited for her to go on.

"They have always told me everything," Stephanie said slowly. "But for the last week or so, they've been whispering a lot. And today they clammed up completely when I walked into the room." Stephanie shook her head and looked worried.

Look for these and other books
in the Sleepover Friends Series:

Stephanie's Family Secret

Susan Saunders

AN
APPLE
PAPERBACK

SCHOLASTIC INC.
New York Toronto London Auckland Sydney

ISBN 0-590-41845-9

Copyright © 1989 by Daniel Weiss Associates, Inc. All rights reserved. Published by Scholastic Inc. APPLE PAPERBACKS is a registered trademark of Scholastic Inc. SLEEPOVER FRIENDS is a trademark of Scholastic Inc.

12 11 10 9 8 7 6 5 4 3 2 1   9/8 0 1 2 3 4/9

Printed in the U.S.A.   28

First Scholastic printing, April 1989

Chapter 1

It was almost time to go home on a Friday afternoon. Mrs. Mead was taking down the names of people who wanted to be in the Riverhurst Elementary School fifth-grade talent show. Since I intended to stay as far away from it as I could, I was mostly reading a story in the latest issue of *Star Turns*, which I had hidden under the top of my desk.

I listened with a corner of my ear as Mark Freedman told Mrs. Mead he'd play his drums. Then Steven Gitten said he'd juggle. Karla Stamos raised her hand and declared, "Mrs. Mead, I'd like to do a selection from my latest ballet recital."

Karla's okay, but she's kind of dull — her mother must have decided ballet would make her more interesting, or at least less klutzy. Karla hardly

1

ever wears anything that isn't brown. I wondered if her ballet outfit would be brown, too.

I turned the page of my movie magazine as silently as I could, reading that Kevin DeSpain — who happens to be my favorite actor — "just jetted to Monte Carlo to begin work on his next picture in which he plays an international jewel thief." I'd hand over my pearl ring to Kevin DeSpain anytime, and my silver bracelet, too, I said to myself. There was an entry blank at the end of the article: "Win an evening with Kevin! Dine with him at his favorite eatery in L.A. Take a moonlit walk on the beach at Malibu." A whiny voice cut into my thoughts. Just about then, Kate Beekman poked me hard with her elbow. Kate sits next to me in 5B; she's my oldest friend. She wanted to make sure I knew that Jenny Carlin was speaking. "I'll play a clarinet solo, Mrs. Mead — 'Moon Over Miami,' " Jenny said as sweetly as she could, batting her eyelashes toward the left side of the room, where Pete Stone sits.

Kate raised an eyebrow at me, and we grinned. We'd heard Jenny play at a band concert. The only thing squeakier than Jenny's voice is her clarinet.

Henry Larkin and Larry Jackson said they'd do some magic tricks, and Robin Becker said she'd play the piano.

I'd gone back to reading my magazine, so I didn't see Stephanie Green waving her arm, even though she sits right in front of Kate and me. I didn't look up until I heard her say, "Mrs. Mead, Kate Beekman, Lauren Hunter, Patti Jenkins, and I . . ."

My stomach went into a free-fall — I'm Lauren Hunter — and I heard Patti's gasp, all the way from the back row. Kate gave the leg of Stephanie's chair a ferocious kick, but there was no stopping her. ". . . are going to do something together," Stephanie went on. "We'll let you know exactly *what* next week."

"Stephanie!" I hissed, letting *Star Turns* slide off my lap and onto the floor.

"Fine," said Mrs. Mead, writing us down. "Lauren, is that a magazine I see?"

Luckily, the bell rang just then and saved me. Under cover of all the kids in class jumping up and milling around, I made a dive for *Star Turns* and stuffed it into my backpack. Then I hurried out of the room after Stephanie, Kate, and Patti.

We all caught up with Stephanie at the bicycle rack in front of the school building. "I can't believe you volunteered all four of us for Amateur Night!" Kate said accusingly. "Are you out of your gourd?"

"It'll be fun," Stephanie replied breezily, pulling

her bike out of the rack. "Practically everybody else in fifth grade is doing it."

"All the boys, you mean," Kate said. "Mark, Larry, Kyle . . . *Steven*." Stephanie thinks Steven Gitten is really cute, since he grew two inches and got his hair cut short. Kate went on, "I can't sing, I can't play a musical instrument . . . I'm not even any good at telling jokes. There couldn't be a worse idea — could there, Lauren?"

"I get such stage fright I can't even remember my own name," I said. I felt queasy just thinking about it.

"We'll do something easy," Stephanie said. "It's for a good cause."

"The class trip to Washington . . . ," Patti Jenkins said dreamily. Patti's one of the smartest kids in school, and she loves museums, which Washington is full of. I guess the idea of all those museums balanced the fear of being onstage for her.

"We have *plenty* of time to make money for the class trip," I pointed out. "We could have a garage sale, or wash cars, or clean out basements. . . ."

"Are you going to let Jenny Carlin show you up, Lauren?" Stephanie interrupted cagily.

"I couldn't care less what Jenny Carlin does," I said huffily. "As long as she leaves me — "

4

Kate cut me off. "I know tons about movies, Lauren and Patti are both good at sports, Patti's the smartest kid at school, and you're great at shopping, Stephanie. But that doesn't exactly make us entertainers, does it?" She climbed on her bike and started pedaling up the hill. "You'd better get us out of this before we make total jerks of ourselves for two dollars and fifty cents a ticket."

Stephanie rolled into the street behind Kate, shaking her head and smiling smugly. "No need — I've thought of something we can do that takes practically no talent at all."

Once Stephanie makes up her mind, she's like a bulldozer. "Sounds perfect," I said glumly.

"What is it?" Patti asked, pedaling faster until she was even with Stephanie and me.

"What doesn't take talent?" I said.

"Yeah — are we going to doze onstage? Or maybe just breathe?" said Kate.

"No, we'll lip synch to a record!" Stephanie said. "I've even got a great name for us: The Four Aces!"

"This gets worse and worse!" Kate moaned. "The four of us standing there in front of the whole school *and* their parents, moving our mouths like dummies. . . ."

5

"We won't be just *standing* there," Stephanie said. "I'll work out some steps for us."

"You think jumping around while we move our mouths is going to improve things?" Kate exclaimed. "No way!" And she waited for me to agree with her.

I thought about being onstage, with hundreds of eyes zeroed in on me, and I shuddered. But then I thought of the big smirk on Jenny Carlin's face when we chickened out. . . . "Stephanie said we'd do it, so I think we have to," I answered at last.

Stephanie nodded approvingly. "Patti?"

"If Lauren will . . . I guess I will," Patti said.

"Come on, Kate," Stephanie coaxed. "The four of us are a team, aren't we?"

"One for all, and all for one?" I stuck in.

"That was the *Three* Musketeers, Lauren," Kate said. "Not *four*. I've seen the movie a hundred times."

"You know what I mean," I muttered. The four of us do everything together.

Actually, there weren't always four of us — not even three. At first, it was just Kate and me. We've lived practically next door to each other on Pine Street for our whole lives — there's only one house between us. Kate and I started playing together while

6

we were still in diapers, and by kindergarten we were best friends. That's when our sleepovers began. Every Friday night, either I'd sleep over at Kate's house, or she'd sleep over at mine. Kate's dad, Dr. Beekman, named us the Sleepover Twins.

In those days, a sleepover meant making Kool-Pops in ice-cube trays, and melting S'mores in the toaster oven. Kate and I would dress up in our moms' clothes and play Grown-Ups or Let's Pretend.

As we got older, our cooking improved — Kate started making her special marshmallow fluff super-fudge, and I invented my onion-soup-olives-bacon-bits-and-sour-cream dip. Besides eating bushels of barbecue potato chips and drinking gallons of Dr Pepper, we had Kate's little sister, Melissa the Monster, to avoid at Kate's house, and my older brother, Roger, and his friends to spy on at mine. We watched every movie on Friday-night TV — Kate wants to be a movie director some day — made up our own Mad Libs, and played a zillion games of Truth or Dare.

Those sleepovers have really added up — Kate and I have spent thousands of hours with each other over the years. You'd think we'd be a lot alike after all the time together, but that couldn't be less true. Besides looking totally different — I'm tall and brown-haired, Kate's short and blonde — Kate's ex-

tra neat, and I'm always messy. Kate's sensible —
she thinks things through. I'll have to admit, I jump
to conclusions. She makes me pull myself together,
and I loosen her up a little.

I believe our differences are one of the reasons
we've always gotten along. And maybe the reason
Kate and Stephanie didn't hit it off at first is that
they're too much alike. At least, that's what my
brother always said: "Of course they fight — they're
both bossy!"

The summer before fourth grade, Stephanie
moved from the city to a new house at the other end
of Pine Street. She and I got to be friends because
we sat next to each other in 4A, Mr. Civello's class.

Stephanie told neat stories about her life back
in the city. She also knew all the latest dance steps,
and she already had her own style of dressing — she
was the only fourth-grader who always wore red,
black, and white. Stephanie was lots of fun, so even-
tually I invited her to a Friday-night sleepover at my
house. I wanted Kate to get to know her, too.

The sleepover was a disaster! Kate thought
Stephanie was a big show-off, because Stephanie
was always going on about the city. And Stephanie
thought Kate was much too serious.

Still, I didn't give up. When Stephanie invited

8

me to a sleepover at her house, I asked if Kate could come, too. Mrs. Green's peanut-butter chocolate-chip cookies improved everyone's mood, and we watched a triple-feature on Stephanie's private TV set. She's an only child, so she has her own TV, her own VCR, and her own phone.

Pretty soon, Kate, Stephanie, and I started riding our bikes back and forth to school as a group, since all three of us live on Pine Street. We'd hang around together some Saturdays, too. Little by little, the Sleepover Twins became a threesome.

Not that Kate and Stephanie were suddenly in total agreement. They still argued plenty, and I found myself caught in the middle more often than not . . . until Patti Jenkins turned up in our fifth-grade class. Patti's from the city, too. In fact, she and Stephanie had actually gone to the same city school for a couple of years.

Patti's kind and thoughtful, and Kate and I both liked her right away. It wasn't long before there were *four* Sleepover Friends.

We'd braked our bikes at the corner of Pine Street. "So," Stephanie said to Kate, "are you with us or not? The *Three* Aces doesn't make any sense."

Kate sighed loudly. "Oh, all right!" she said.

9

"Great," said Stephanie. "I'll bring over some tapes tonight. We can choose a song and start practicing our routine. What time do you want us?"

That Friday the sleepover was at Kate's house.

"Six-thirty or so," Kate said. "Dad's going to drive us to get take-out as soon as he's home from the hospital."

"What kind of take-out?" Stephanie asked.

"Mexican, I think — from that new place, Pancho's Villa," Kate answered.

"Excellent!" Stephanie said. "Mexican's my favorite! See you later with the tapes." She pedaled down Pine Street.

Patti waved good-bye, too, heading toward her house on Mill Road.

Kate frowned at me and shook her head. "Stephanie's done it again," she said.

"One good thing," I said, trying to look on the bright side, "most songs are only about three minutes long."

"Three minutes that will take a lifetime to live down," Kate said gloomily as she turned into her driveway.

Chapter 2

"It never feels as though our sleepovers have officially started until all four of us are here," I said to Kate and Patti that evening. We were sitting on the floor of Kate's bedroom, surrounded by cartons of take-out, two king-size bottles of Dr Pepper, plates, glasses, bowls, and a big stack of paper napkins — Mexican food can be *very* messy. "What time did Stephanie say she was coming?"

"Around eight-thirty. And don't hog all the taco dip, Lauren," Kate scolded, snatching the white cardboard container away before I could lower a tortilla chip into it. "Give some to Patti."

"There's plenty for everybody," I protested. I have what *I* call a healthy appetite and everybody else calls "the bottomless pit."

11

"That's okay, Kate — I've got all I can eat," Patti said quickly. She pointed to her plate, which looked almost as full as it had been when Kate dished out the food. Patti wasn't enjoying her dinner from Pancho's Villa as much as I was.

Making a face at Kate, I grabbed the taco dip again. "Stephanie's going to be really sorry she missed this," I said, scooping up more dip on a chip. Stephanie's appetite is almost as healthy as mine.

"What exactly did she say when she called you, Kate?" Patti asked.

"Something about her parents acting weird — you know, whispering and stuff," Kate replied. "And that she wanted to have dinner with them, to try and find out what's up."

Patti murmured, "The last time my parents acted weird, it was because they'd decided we were moving to Alaska. I hope it's nothing like that." Patti's parents are both history professors at the university, and not too long ago, they were offered jobs in Anchorage. We thought we were going to lose the newest Sleepover Friend.

I shook my head. "I don't think the Greens are moving anywhere," I said. "Mr. Green told me last month that he'd bought a lifetime membership to the Health Club on Main."

12

Mr. Green knows I'm into sports and exercising, because he sees me jogging around the neighborhood with Roger. Poor man — his own daughter's about as interested in getting sweaty as she is in falling off a cliff.

"I'll bet they're planning a surprise for Stephanie," Kate said, dropping another spoonful of refried beans onto her plate.

"Like when they got her the VCR," I remembered. Kate was probably right — Stephanie's parents were always coming up with neat gifts for her. "Being an only child definitely has its advantages," I added.

"You said it!" Kate muttered, pointing at her closed door. Melissa had started pounding on the other side of it. "Get out of here!" Kate yelled.

"I just came to tell you Stephanie's out front, Creep-o!" Melissa shouted back. She gave Kate's door an angry thump before she stomped down the hall.

"Stephanie's here!" The three of us scrambled to our feet and raced downstairs. Kate flung open the front door just as Stephanie reached for the knocker. Her dad beeped his horn at us and pulled away from the curb.

"What's going on with your parents?" I blurted

13

out as soon as Stephanie had stepped inside.

"You're not moving, are you?" Patti asked anxiously, before Stephanie had time to answer.

"I told Lauren and Patti your parents just wanted to surprise you with a present," said Kate. "Was I right?"

Stephanie put her finger to her lips and nodded in the direction of the kitchen, where Dr. and Mrs. Beekman and Melissa were having their dinner. "Let's go to your room first," she murmured.

As soon as Kate had shut her door behind us, Stephanie flopped down on the bed and groaned.

"What's all the mystery?" I asked.

"That's just it," Stephanie replied. "I don't know. I thought they'd tell me at dinner. . . ." She shook her head and looked worried.

Kate, Patti, and I waited for her to go on.

"My parents have always told me everything," Stephanie said slowly. "They think a family should talk things out. But for the last week or so, they've been whispering a lot. And today they clammed up completely when I walked into the room."

"They're getting you a present," Kate insisted. "Something major" — she thought for a moment — "like a swimming pool!"

Stephanie shook her head. "I don't think so,"

she said. "Daddy joined the health club so we could swim there. And usually if they're planning a surprise, like the VCR and the movie tapes, there are plenty of hints beforehand. You know, 'Stephanie, if you were choosing your five favorite movies, what would they be?' And they beam a lot." Stephanie frowned. "There certainly hasn't been any beaming going on in the last few days — mom and dad seem kind of distracted." She sat up and shrugged her shoulders. "You know what I think it is?" she said finally.

"What?" Kate, Patti, and I said together.

"Remember that old movie we saw a couple of Fridays ago — *Time of Our Lives*?" Stephanie asked.

"Sure — that's the one where the guy loses his job . . . ," I began, but I stopped myself to stare at Stephanie.

Stephanie looked straight back at me. "That's it," she said softly.

"You mean your father lost his job?" Patti said, much louder than usual.

Stephanie nodded sadly. "Has to be."

I couldn't imagine Mr. Green getting fired! He's a lawyer — the Greens moved to Riverhurst in the first place because Mr. Green was offered a terrific job at the biggest law firm here: Blake, Binder, and

Rosten. He dresses in nice-looking gray suits and blue shirts, and he works long hours, just like successful lawyers on TV shows.

"Stephanie, you're jumping to conclusions!" Kate exclaimed. "That's Lauren's specialty," she added with a smile. She and Stephanie are always teasing me about letting my imagination run away with me.

When Stephanie didn't smile back, though, Kate said, "What makes you so sure?"

"A couple of weeks ago Dad mentioned that he had a big meeting with his boss coming up. I think he must have had that meeting last week, and it was bad news."

The three of us didn't say anything for a minute. Then Kate asked, "You haven't got any proof . . . have you?"

"No," Stephanie admitted. "But that's where you guys can help me."

"How?" I asked.

"You remember in the movie, the man didn't want to upset his kids by telling them he'd lost his job," Stephanie said. "So he'd wake up early every morning and get dressed like he was going to his office?"

The three of us nodded.

16

"Then, instead of going to his office, he'd hang out in the library all day and come home at the regular time, as though he'd had a full day at work?" Stephanie went on.

"Right — and while he was in the library, he read lots of books about inventions and came up with an invention of his own and sold it and made tons of money and. . . ." I got carried away by the story.

"Lauren!" Kate said sternly. "So?" she said to Stephanie.

"So, Monday morning we follow my dad on our bikes and see where he goes!" Stephanie said. "I'd do it by myself, but I can't pedal as fast as you and Patti can, Lauren."

"We'll be late for school!" Kate protested. She's never late for anything.

"Not necessarily," Stephanie replied. "Daddy leaves for work early, around eight-fifteen. I think we'll have plenty of time to follow him and still get back to school before the bell."

Kate tried again. "Why don't you just call his office? If they say he doesn't work there anymore — "

"What if he's asked the secretary who answers the phone not to tell anyone, yet?" Stephanie said.

"She'll make something up . . . ," Patti said.

"Exactly," Stephanie said grimly.

I thought about how awful I'd feel if my dad had lost his job at Blaney Real Estate. "I'll do it," I told Stephanie.

"Me, too," Patti said.

"Okay, okay," said Kate crossly. "But only to prove you're imagining things, Stephanie."

"I hope you're right," Stephanie said. But she sounded a little better. She looked down at the cartons of Mexican food spread out on the floor of Kate's room. "Is there any taco dip left? I didn't *really* enjoy my dinner."

Chapter
3

After Stephanie had eaten enough to catch up with us, we listened to her tapes and chose a song for the talent show — "I Wanna Be Your Girl," by the Polka Dots.

"Only three minutes and ten seconds of fatal embarrassment," Kate murmured to me.

Then Stephanie lined us up. "Lauren and Patti in the middle. . . ."

"Shouldn't we rest for an hour or so — let our food settle?" I moaned, hugging my enchilada-stuffed stomach. "Dancing is a lot like swimming, isn't it? What if I get a cramp?"

"Don't worry — we'll save you," Kate said.

"Lauren and Patti in the middle, because you're tall and skinny, although I don't know why *you're* skinny, Lauren, because you eat like a horse!'' Stephanie said. ''And Kate and I on the ends because. . . .''

"Because we're short and fat?'' Kate teased. ''Thanks, Stephanie — I needed that.''

Actually, Kate's not fat at all. Neither is Stephanie, really, but she's always talking about whether or not her face is looking too round, and sucking in her cheeks in front of the mirror, and threatening to go on a diet.

''Because Kate and I are *shorter* is what I was going to say,'' Stephanie went on. ''Okay, we'll work on the chorus first, since it's repeated a lot. I'll play it through a couple of times, just so we can be sure we all know the words.''

Stephanie snapped the tape into Kate's cassette player, and the Polka Dots blasted through the speakers: ''I wanna be your girl, oh, yeah — come on and dance with me. . . .''

We listened to it four times for the words alone, and then about six more times while we worked on the steps, with Stephanie directing: ''On 'girl,' spread your arms out to the sides. Then, on 'come on and dance,' we'll do the moonwalk. Start with your left foot. . . .''

We kept it up until finally Mrs. Beekman knocked on Kate's door. ''Would you mind playing something else for a while, girls? I'm afraid I'll be singing this one in my sleep."

She sang the chorus of "I Wanna Be Your Girl," and we all giggled.

"Sure, Mom." Kate switched off the cassette player. "We were all about to go bananas ourselves."

"Thank you, thank you," Mrs. Beekman sang. "And good night."

"Anyway, it's request time," Kate said to us.

On Friday and Saturday nights, you can call up WBRM, the Riverhurst radio station, and ask them to play a song for somebody. Elementary school kids don't usually call in, but we listen to find out what's going on at the junior high and high school.

"Anybody want some dessert?" Kate asked. "We can microwave one of Mom's fruit squares."

"Sure. Let's get some more Dr Pepper, too," I said. "I'm dying of thirst."

"I'm with you," said Stephanie, wiping her damp forehead with the back of her hand. "I must have lost two pounds at least."

"We'll take the radio with us." Kate opened the door to her room and stuck her head out to make sure Melissa was safely in bed. Then we tiptoed downstairs.

Both of Kate's parents are great cooks. One of

my favorite things is digging through the dishes and bowls of leftovers in their refrigerator.

"Can I have one of these, Kate?" I'd uncovered a container of Dr. Beekman's stuffed clams.

"Sure, go ahead," Kate said. "Take whatever you want."

"Sssh!" said Stephanie. "Here's a request. . . ."

"From the girls in 7C to Donald F.," the deejay was saying. " 'My Guy'!"

"Oh, no!" we all groaned. "Not Donald!"

Donald Foster lives in the house between Kate's and mine. He is without doubt the vainest boy in the seventh grade, and possibly in all of Riverhurst.

"He's going to get so fat-headed that he won't be able to fit through doors," Kate said.

"Neither will Lauren," said Stephanie as I stuck a spoon into a blue bowl heaped with mashed potatoes and popped it in my mouth.

"Stop!" came a shriek from the hall. Melissa hurtled into the kitchen.

"Were you spying on us?" Kate growled as her little sister snatched the bowl away from me.

"Mommy!" Melissa howled. "Lauren's eating my map!"

Urk! I clutched my stomach. "Map?" I repeated

anxiously. The mashed potatoes *had* tasted kind of strange. . . .

Stephanie and Patti were staring at me as though they expected me to keel over, but Kate burst out laughing.

"Melissa — what's wrong?" Mrs. Beekman stumbled sleepily down the stairs and into the kitchen.

"Lauren's out d-done herself," Kate stammered through her giggles. "She gobbled up several states!"

Seeing my sickly expression, Mrs. Beekman said reassuringly, "It won't hurt you, Lauren — it's just flour, a lot of salt, and water, for Melissa's class's relief map of the country."

"She ate so much we probably won't be able to make Texas!" Melissa grumbled.

"We'll mix up some more dough tomorrow," Mrs. Beekman promised. "Now get back to bed, Melissa, and leave the girls alone. Good night again," she told us. Yawning, she steered Melissa toward the stairs.

Even Patti had started to giggle by then.

"How much salt?" I asked Kate, and swallowed hard.

"If you were thirsty before. . . ." Kate handed

me an entire king-size bottle of Dr Pepper.

"The Monster Who Ate Texas!" Stephanie cracked up.

"Very funny!" I muttered, pouring myself a huge glass of soda and chugging it down. Who knew the refrigerator was booby-trapped?

"Let's watch some *Chiller Theater*," Kate suggested. "It's *Return of the Vampire*, and — "

"Listen," Stephanie interrupted.

". . . for Steven G. in 5B, from a secret admirer!" the deejay boomed as Stephanie turned up the volume. " 'Like to Get to Know You Better.' "

"Steven G. in 5B!" Stephanie, Kate, Patti, and I said at the same time.

"If you weren't here, Stephanie, I'd think the secret admirer was you," Kate added.

"But I *am* here, so who is it?" said Stephanie.

"Uh. . . ." Patti looked thoughtful. "Maybe . . ."

"Yes?" the rest of us said.

"This afternoon after school, when I was riding up the hill behind you guys," Patti said, "I noticed Steven talking to Jenny Carlin near the side steps."

"Jenny Carlin!" Stephanie exclaimed. "What about Pete Stone?"

"Jenny's been ignoring him lately," Kate said, pouring more Dr Pepper into my glass. "I saw her

24

cut him dead in the cafeteria yesterday."

I'd thought Jenny was batting her eyelashes at Pete in class that day, but Steven Gitten sits on the left side of the room, too. . . .

"I know how we could make sure," Kate said.

"How?" Stephanie asked.

"One of us could call her — " Kate began.

"And say, 'Hi, Jenny — this is Stephanie Green. Did you just request a song for Steven?' " Stephanie said. "I'm sure she'd love to share all her secrets with us!"

"Of course not! Whoever was calling could say she was Marcy Gitten" — Marcy is Steven's little sister, a third-grader — "and tell Jenny that Steven wanted to know!" said Kate.

"Good thinking!" said Stephanie. "Who's going to do it?"

"Who sounds the most like a little kid?" said Kate. She and Stephanie both stared straight at me.

"Uh-uh! No way! Not me!" Okay, so I have the kind of voice that makes me sound about six years old on the telephone. Why should I have to call up my worst enemy? "Besides, it's too late," I said. "Jenny's probably gone to bed."

"She has not — not if she just called in a request," Kate pointed out. "I'll bet Angela's spending

25

the night with her, too." Angela Kemp is Jenny's sidekick.

"Come on, Lauren," Stephanie pleaded. "I'll let you borrow my black jacket for a whole week." Stephanie has a great-looking black leather jacket with red trim on it.

"Oh, all right!" I said. "What's her number?"

Kate pulled the phone book off the counter and flipped through it. "Carlin . . . Carlin . . . doesn't she live on River Drive?"

Stephanie nodded. "She's bragged about it often enough." River Drive is one of the most expensive neighborhoods in Riverhurst.

"Six, four, three, four, two, eight, seven," Kate read out loud.

I picked up the wall phone and pushed the buttons. "If her parents answer, I'm hanging up," I warned as it rang.

But Jenny answered on the first ring. "Hello?" she said kind of breathlessly.

I raised my voice even higher than usual. "Hello — is Jenny Carlin there?" I practically squeaked.

"This is Jenny Carlin," Jenny said. "Who is this?"

"Marcy Gitten," I said.

"Marcy Gitten!" Jenny almost shouted. "It's Marcy Gitten!" she repeated to someone there, undoubtedly Angela.

"Mmm-hmm. Steven told me to call you. . . ." Kate, Stephanie, and Patti held their hands over their mouths, trying not to laugh at the face I had to make to talk so high. ". . . to call you about the request on WBRM. I'm not sure what that means . . . ," I added, trying to sound like a third-grader and ending up sounding like a dork.

"What did Steven say about the request?" Jenny asked, so excitedly that I felt myself starting to lose my grip, too.

"He . . . He . . . hee-hee-hee!" I couldn't help it. I burst into giggles, too, so I clicked off.

"Did she do it?" Stephanie asked.

"She must have, because she — " I was saying when the Beekmans' phone rang.

"Grab it!" Kate hissed. "Before it wakes up my parents!"

As soon as I picked up the phone, Jenny Carlin's voice squawked out of the receiver: "I know that was one of you! And I just have one thing to say: I don't get mad — *I get even!*"

Chapter 4

The plan for Monday morning was to leave our houses just after eight, telling our parents we had to get to school early. Stephanie said that would give us plenty of time to get into position, since her dad usually drives to work around eight-fifteen.

We'd hide ourselves and our bikes in the hedge at the corner of Pine Street and Hillcrest, which is the road Mr. Green takes to the office and is also the road that runs in front of Riverhurst Elementary School. We'd stay in the hedge until Mr. Green had driven past us and turned the corner onto Hillcrest. Then we'd race after him.

"It might be a good idea to let a car or two get between us and Dad," Stephanie said when she

28

called Sunday night. "We don't want him to spot us in his rearview mirror. And maybe we should wear caps or something for a disguise, just in case he does see us."

"Are your parents still acting weird?" I said.

"Weirder than ever," said Stephanie. "They were looking at a book together this afternoon in the den. When I walked through the door, Mom stuffed the book between the couch cushions."

"You didn't even see the cover?" I asked her.

"It was light blue . . . no, maybe it was pink. Something pale," Stephanie said. "Anyway, I sneaked back into the den later to find the book, but it was gone. I bet it was something about job-hunting. Or how to live on five dollars a day."

"I'm sure it wasn't anything like that," I said quickly. But something was definitely going on with Stephanie's parents. . . .

The next morning, I set my alarm for a quarter to seven instead of seven. I'm pretty slow when I wake up, and I wanted to give myself plenty of time to get ready.

Our doorbell rang at eight o'clock on the dot. "There's Kate!" I said, swallowing the last spoonful of my cereal.

"Have a good day, honey," my father said. He's

29

not as perfect a dresser as Mr. Green, but he's cute.

"See you this afternoon, sweetie," my mother said.

On my way out, I grabbed Roger's baseball cap off the hall table and jammed it on my head.

When I opened the front door, I burst out laughing. "What are you supposed to be?" I asked Kate. She was wearing her father's old fishing hat, with a couple of lures stuck in the brim, and a huge pair of dark glasses.

Kate grinned. "Stephanie wanted a disguise."

"You look like Fisherman Frank on Channel 21," I told her. "Only cleaner." Fisherman Frank is the host of the most boring program on television — he just sits in a boat and fishes. He's always covered with fish scales, and he digs around in rusty cans of worms and slimy bait buckets.

"Happy trolling," said Kate, which is Fisherman Frank's sign-off. "Go get your bike."

We pedaled up Pine Street to the corner in front of the Norrises' house. Then we peered around to see if anyone was watching us. When we were sure there was no one in sight, and no faces in any windows, we rolled our bikes into the old lilac hedge that separates the Norrises' yard from the street.

"Hi," a voice whispered from further down the hedge.

"Patti, is that you?" I whispered back. Through all the leaves and branches, I could just make out a head covered with a knitted cap in the university colors, red and blue.

"Yes," Patti replied softly. "I can't get to you, though, unless I crawl out first. It's too brushy."

"Stay where you are," Kate whispered to her. We shouldn't be here long — it's almost eight-ten."

Where was Stephanie?

Kate and I crouched in the hedge and watched Mr. Norris back his car out of their garage. Next Mrs. Norris came out to walk their dog, Barney. He's a standard poodle who weighs about eighty pounds. Kate and I had to giggle, because he drags Mrs. Norris all over the place. We heard Patti giggling, too.

Not long after that, my dad's old car clanked past, and then Mr. and Mrs. Foster's station wagon. I started to get uncomfortable. "It's kind of damp in here," I murmured.

Patti sneezed twice.

"My feet are soaked," Kate grumbled. "Where is Stephanie?"

And where was Mr. Green? He couldn't have

gone to work any other way, because Hillcrest leads straight to Main Street, which is where his office is. Was it possible he wasn't going to work at all?

The school bus stopped at the end of the Norrises' sidewalk, and the two little Norris girls, Samantha and Lolly, climbed aboard.

"Eight-twenty," Kate muttered. "If he's not here in two more minutes, I'm leaving!"

One minute and fifty seconds later, Stephanie came crashing into the hedge about two feet from Kate and me. She was wearing a red-and-black beret to match her red, black, and white sweater. This was a disguise?

"Where have you been?" Kate wanted to know.

"Sssh!" said Stephanie. "Donald's right behind. . . ."

"Hey, girls — what are you up to now?" Donald Foster poked his blond head into the hedge and grinned at us. "Hide-and-seek?"

Since Donald's house is between Kate's and mine, he's been a witness to all kinds of strange sleepover happenings, like the time we couldn't wash the purple styling gel out of our hair because a water main on Pine Street had broken.

"Very funny!" I whispered.

"Go away, Donald!" Kate hissed.

"Truth or Dare, right?" Donald guessed — he's also been on the receiving end of several of our sleepover Truth or Dare games. "Or is it a new way of playing hooky?"

Donald was showing no signs of leaving. I think he just can't believe there are any girls in the world who wouldn't rather gaze into his big blue eyes than do anything else.

"Donald, please . . . ," Stephanie begged. "Dad could be coming down Pine Street any second now!" she said to Kate and me.

I pushed forward through the hedge so that Donald would have to back up. "Give us a break, okay?" I said to him. "This is serious, Donald," I added in a low voice, nodding toward Stephanie, who looked really worried.

"Okay, okay." Donald set his skateboard down on the pavement. "See you around."

I waited until he was coasting down Hillcrest. Then I squeezed back into the lilacs.

"He was sitting at the dining room table when I finally left, filling out stacks of papers," Stephanie was saying to Kate and Patti, who'd pushed closer.

"Your dad? What kind of papers?" I asked.

"*I* don't know," Stephanie said crossly. "Nobody tells me anything anymore."

33

Kate glanced at her watch. "It's almost time for the first bell."

One bell rings at eight thirty-five to get us into the school building. The second bell rings at eight forty-five, and if you're not in your desk by then, you're late.

Kate had never been late to school in her life, and I knew she didn't want to start. Patti looked as nervous as I felt — she and I had already been late once. Two tardies and you get to spend lunchtime in the principal's office.

"Come on, guys — I need you!" Stephanie murmured.

"Here comes a car!" Patti said suddenly.

We peered through the leaves as a blue car slowed down near the intersection — Stephanie's dad's car is blue.

"It's him!" Stephanie hissed.

34

Chapter 5

Mr. Green was turning the corner onto Hillcrest. Without another word, Stephanie shoved her bike out of the lilac hedge, jumped on it, and sped after him.

Kate, Patti, and I looked at each other. I was pretty sure we were all thinking the same thing: Whether or not Stephanie was right about her dad's problems, this was really important to her, a lot more important than our being late to school, or even having to spend lunch hour in Mrs. Wainwright's office. At the exact time, the three of us pushed our bikes out of the hedge and tore after Stephanie.

Hillcrest runs downhill all the way past our school, so Stephanie wasn't having any trouble keeping up with her father's car. In fact, her main trouble seemed to be staying out of sight. When Mr. Green stopped at the first red light, Stephanie almost fell over, skidding out of range behind a parked car.

Patti, Kate, and I slowed down until the light changed and Mr. Green got going again. After a silver van had pulled in behind Mr. Green's blue two-door, we started pedaling faster, and glided up to Stephanie.

"This is easier than I thought it would be," she said. "I'm not even sweaty." As I said before, Stephanie's not crazy about vigorous exercise.

"Duck. Here comes the school," Kate warned.

The first bell had already rung, but there were a few kids who'd just been driven up in their parents' cars. It was our rotten luck that one of them had to be Jenny Carlin!

Jenny had climbed out of her car and was saying good-bye to her mother while the four of us, in our strange assortment of hats, were pedaling toward the school. Jenny stopped talking and stared.

We were almost even with the front sidewalk when we saw her rush toward Mrs. Dailey, the monitor. As we streaked past, Jenny pointed at us.

"That does it!" Kate said grimly. "It'll be all over the school in three seconds."

"You guys can quit now and still not be late," Stephanie told us. "I can manage."

But Mr. Green had hit the other side of the twenty-mile-an-hour school zone and speeded up. That's about where Hillcrest slopes uphill again, too. There was no way Stephanie, with her short legs, would be able to keep up with him.

"You can go back," I said to Kate, "but I'm staying." I started pedaling faster.

"So am I," said Patti.

"All for one," said Kate with a sigh.

Patti and I had trained for the Bike-a-Thon together, and we were still in pretty good shape. We'd pulled away from Stephanie and Kate before they were halfway up the hill.

The traffic grew heavier as we got closer to Main. It was becoming much more likely that we would lose Mr. Green than that he would spot us.

"I think he's turning!" Patti called out over the rumble of car and truck engines. "To the left at the next block — his blinker's on."

We had to wait for a lot of traffic to clear out of the intersection before we could cross the street ourselves. Then we raced down Columbine after Mr. Green's blue car.

"I don't know where Stephanie and Kate are," Patti said, glancing back over her shoulder. "I hope they saw us make the turn."

But we couldn't worry about them then. Mr. Green drove pretty fast for five blocks straight. Then he made a right onto Sills.

"Maybe he's going to Main Street after all," I said to Patti — Sills runs into Main. We were both starting to puff a little.

"He's already passed the Blake, Binder, and Rosten block, though," Patti pointed out. Their office is only a couple of buildings past the intersection of Hillcrest and Main Street, and we were five or six blocks east of that. And when Mr. Green pulled out onto Main Street, he turned left again, not right, toward his office.

"He's slowing down," Patti said. "Thank goodness."

The two of us steered behind an old gray panel truck as Mr. Green slipped into a parking space across the street, in front of the First National Bank and next to the Riverhurst Free Library.

"Oh, no!" Patti groaned. "The library!"

"I have a horrible feeling Stephanie was right," I said.

We could see Mr. Green checking his watch.

38

Then he rolled down his window and just sat there.

"Now what?" Patti said. We'd climbed off our bikes and crouched down behind the truck.

"If Stephanie and Kate tear around the corner onto Main, Mr. Green's very likely to spot them," I said.

Patti nodded. "You keep an eye on him, and I'll head them off." Still stooping to stay out of sight, Patti rolled her bike down the sidewalk until she was out of Mr. Green's rearview mirror range. Then she climbed on and shot around the corner.

I sat down on the curb and waited. And waited. I watched the minute hand on the old clock on top of the bank building inch its way from eight fifty-five, to eight fifty-six, to eight fifty-seven, to eight fifty-eight. No Patti or Stephanie or Kate, and Mr. Green didn't move. We were going to be so late to school that a lunch hour in Mrs. Wainwright's office seemed like a picnic to me. We'd probably be *living* in her office for the rest of the year.

Eight fifty-nine. . . . As the minute hand lined up with the 12, Mr. Green opened the car door. He reached into the backseat to pick up his briefcase. Then he climbed out of the car and slammed the door closed.

39

There he goes, into the library . . . , I was thinking.

But I was totally wrong. Mr. Green walked straight up the steps of the First National Bank and disappeared through the revolving doors!

Where are you guys when I need you? I complained silently to Stephanie, Patti, and Kate. Then I shrugged and stood up. I locked my bike to a parking meter and crossed the street. I was supposed to keep an eye on him, wasn't I?

I pulled Roger's baseball cap down low and walked slowly up the long flight of stone steps. Then I peered into the bank through the glass of the revolving doors.

The First National Bank of Riverhurst is very old-fashioned. It has a huge lobby with a very high ceiling, big brass chandeliers, stone pillars, and a black-and-white marble floor. I could see Mr. Green striding across the squares toward the offices at the back of the bank.

If I followed him, he might see me. But if I didn't follow him, we'd never know which office he'd visited. I was trying to decide what to do when someone behind me shoved against the revolving doors. The doors spun me around and dumped me out inside the lobby.

I must have looked a little dizzy, because the man who'd pushed the doors said, "Are you okay, son?"

I *am* tall and kind of thin, but "son"? Undoubtedly my disguise! "Just fine," I whispered, straightening Roger's baseball cap and sidling behind a pillar.

Mr. Green had stopped in front of the first desk to talk to the receptionist. She smiled at him and nodded. Then she picked up her telephone and said a few words. She put the phone down again, stood up, and led Mr. Green between several rows of desks to a closed door. She opened the door, and Mr. Green stepped inside.

That's that, I said to myself. I looked up at the large brass clock at the top of the lobby: nine-ten. Mrs. Mead was already halfway through math, and that's my best class!

I'd hurried out of the bank and was starting down the steps when someone called softly, "Lauren — over here!"

Patti, Stephanie, and Kate were huddled next to my bike. "Where have you been?" Kate asked crossly when I'd dashed across the street to them. She was still wearing the dark glasses, but not Fisherman Frank's hat.

41

"Where have *you* been?" I answered.

"We lost you guys when you turned off Hillcrest. We'd still be riding around if Patti hadn't found us," Kate replied.

"Where's my dad?" Stephanie wanted to know. "In the library?"

I shook my head. "No, in the bank."

"The bank!" Stephanie exclaimed. "Are you sure?"

"I followed him in," I told her. "He went into an office at the back."

"Maybe he's looking for a job . . . ," Stephanie said. "What kind of office?"

"I don't know," I said. "There's some writing on the door, but I was too far away to read it, and I was afraid to get any closer."

"We have to find out," Stephanie said.

"Do you know what time it is?" said Kate, showing Stephanie her watch. "Nine twenty!"

"Ten more minutes won't make things any worse," Stephanie said, starting across the street.

"Right — you can only die once," Kate muttered.

All three of us marched up the steps behind Stephanie and into the First National Bank.

"I love this floor," Stephanie murmured. "How

do you think black-and-white marble would look in a house?" But she snapped back to the problem at hand. "Which door, Lauren?" she asked when we'd stopped behind my pillar.

"That one, through those desks and to the left," I said.

"I can't read it from here, either," Stephanie said, squinting. Neither could Patti, nor Kate, even with her glasses, which she only uses on special occasions. "We'll have to get closer," Stephanie decided.

"Don't you think that receptionist is going to wonder what four kids are doing, hanging around a bank lobby?" I said.

"We'll tell her we're thinking of opening an account," Stephanie said, squaring her shoulders and heading toward the back of the bank. "If Dad comes out, run for it!"

"May I help you, girls?" the receptionist asked. She was young, with short, curly hair and a nice smile. "Ms. Jessup," the name plate on her desk said.

"Our club is interested in opening an account here," Stephanie said. "Can you tell us how we'd go about it?"

"Certainly," said Ms. Jessup. "First, to open an account with this bank, you must deposit at least one hundred dollars. Then you have to fill out some papers, giving your addresses and ages and other information about yourself. . . ."

Fill out papers? That's what Stephanie said Mr. Green had been doing. Maybe he'd just been opening a bank account.

". . . and talk to one of the officers." Ms. Jessup waved her hand at the people sitting behind the other desks.

"Like Mr. Stufano?" Kate asked. That was the name on the door Mr. Green had walked through — we were finally close enough to read it.

"Oh, no — not unless you want to borrow a lot of money," Ms. Jessup said with a smile.

"Borrow a lot of money?" Stephanie repeated blankly.

"That's right," Ms. Jessup replied. "Mr. Stufano is a *loan* officer."

Chapter
6

"A loan officer!" Stephanie croaked.

"I think the door's opening . . . ," Kate warned in a whisper.

The door of Mr. Stufano's office *was* opening a crack. "Ms. Jessup!" a man's deep voice called out.

"Yes, Mr. Stufano?" Ms. Jessup got up and zig-zagged through the rows of desks.

Patti and I started to back away, but Stephanie just stood there, paralyzed.

"Grab her!" Kate hissed at me. She pulled on one of Stephanie's arms, and I pulled on the other. Between us, we more or less dragged Stephanie across the lobby. The four of us hid behind a quick-deposit box.

We were just in time. Ms. Jessup zipped back out of Mr. Stufano's office. She was followed by a tall, balding man with a large stomach — Mr. Stufano? — and Mr. Green! He was nodding, and Mr. Stufano was talking and patting him on the shoulder.

Mr. Stufano had a booming voice, and what he said next absolutely echoed: "You'll be hearing from us about the loan by the end of the week, Ron."

"I can't believe it!" Stephanie moaned. She sank down onto the black-and-white floor. "If my father's borrowing money, it must mean he's been unemployed for weeks already!"

"Maybe it's for a new car," Patti whispered helpfully. "Last year my dad took out a loan to buy the van."

"Both of our cars *are* new," Stephanie said.

Mr. Green and Mr. Stufano shook hands, and Mr. Green headed across the lobby — he walked right past our hideout on his way to the doors. He didn't look like a man with no job. He was wearing a gray suit, a starched blue shirt, and a maroon tie with little yellow stripes, which is the way he always dresses for work. Still, a loan is a loan. . . .

As soon as her dad had sailed through the revolving doors, Stephanie said, "Let's see which way he's going!" She scrambled to her feet and dashed toward the doors, too. But I was ahead of her.

I tried to stop when I got there, to peer through

the glass to make sure it was safe, but Stephanie and Kate and Patti pushed, and I shot onto the top step outside. I'm beginning to feel like a pinball! I thought.

Luckily, Mr. Green was already in his car, looking over his shoulder as he backed out of the parking space. He turned and drove up Main Street.

"I'll bet he's going back home, until it's time for me to get out of school," Stephanie murmured gloomily. She sat down on the top step and sighed.

"What do you want to do now?" Patti asked her.

"How about going to school?" Kate suggested, but Patti and I were focused on Stephanie.

"Why don't we try to raise some money?" I said, sitting down next to Stephanie. "Help your family over this rough spot?"

"How could we raise enough money to make any difference?" Stephanie said, totally discouraged. "Even if we did two parties a weekend. . . ." The four of us have a birthday party business for little kids. Patti and I dress up like clowns and jump around and tell jokes. Kate and Stephanie videotape the whole thing. "Besides," Stephanie went on, "we're still paying off the video camera."

"No, I was thinking about a yard sale," I told her. "The Fosters made four hundred and fifty dollars last summer, just selling junk out of their attic. And what about contests?"

" 'Win an Evening with Kevin DeSpain'?" Kate said, rolling her eyes. She'd been looking at the latest issue of *Star Turns*, too. "Do you know what time it is?" she added.

"There are lots of contests in magazines that let you win actual money," I said. "You've seen them: 'An All-Expense-Paid Trip for Two to Paris on the Concorde, or Five Thousand Dollars in Cash!' And all you have to do is fill out a card and mail it in."

"Usually the drawings are months away, though, aren't they?" Stephanie said. But she sounded kind of interested.

"You guys don't seem to realize we are seriously late . . . ," said Kate.

"Not if you use *old* magazines," I said to Stephanie. "And my mom has tons of them in the basement."

"I could help you go through them," Patti volunteered. "I'm a fast reader."

"I'll return that tweed coat I bought last weekend at Just Juniors — I haven't even taken the tags off," Stephanie said. "That'll definitely save Dad some bucks. And I like the idea of a yard sale, except we couldn't have it at my house. I don't want to upset my parents more by letting them know *I* know."

"Then we'll have it at my house," Kate said. She was starting to believe something serious *was* going on in the Green household, with Stephanie returning clothes she'd bought. "But could we get moving? It's almost ten o'clock!"

"Ten o'clock!" the rest of us exclaimed.

"What happened to your hat?" I asked Kate as we ran down the steps.

"The wind blew it off my head," Kate replied. "The last time I saw it, it was headed south on the front bumper of an oil truck."

"Those were your dad's favorite — " I began as the four of us pedaled like crazy up Main Street.

"Tell me about it!" Kate said glumly. "If Mrs. Wainwright doesn't kill us, Dad will finish me off for losing his best lures."

It was strange riding up to a totally empty school-yard, strange and creepy glancing through the windows and seeing all the kids sitting at their desks while we were outside.

We locked our bikes up at the rack, and Stephanie, Patti, and I pulled off our head gear. Then we raced up the front walk.

"We'll have to get notes from Mrs. Jamison," Patti said. Mrs. Jamison is the school secretary.

"I just hope Mrs. Wainwright is busy," Kate added.

But Mrs. Wainwright was waiting for us — she'd probably been waiting ever since the monitor passed along Jenny Carlin's news. "Good morning, girls," Mrs. Wainwright said as soon as we'd stepped through the door of the outer office. "I'm sure you have an excellent reason for being so late?"

My stomach lurched — I could feel every corn flake from breakfast dancing around. Patti's lips turned white, Kate swallowed hard, and Stephanie stammered, "It's-it's not their f-fault, Mrs. Wainwright. They were helping me out with a personal problem."

Mrs. Wainwright nodded slowly. "What kind of personal problem?" she asked.

Stephanie gulped. "I really can't — can't say."

"It obviously was not a personal problem at home, because Mrs. Dailey saw all four of you speeding past the school at eight-forty this morning," Mrs. Wainwright said sternly.

Knowing I'd been right about Jenny Carlin was small comfort.

Mrs. Wainwright wrote something on a slip of paper. "This is a note to get you into class. However, I will expect all of you back in my office during lunch — at twelve-fifteen on the dot."

"Yes, Mrs. Wainwright," we mumbled together.

She handed the paper to Stephanie, nodded good-bye, and strode into her office.

Mrs. Jamison gave us a small, sympathetic smile, and Kate, Stephanie, Patti, and I stumbled over each other in our eagerness to get out the door.

"I'm sorry, guys," Stephanie whispered as we hurried down the hall.

"I think I can safely say I've never been so humiliated in my life!" Kate muttered.

Things got even worse, though. Our class was in the middle of the science lesson, but when we knocked at the door of 5B, the lesson stopped dead. Everybody turned to stare at us. You could have heard a pin drop as Stephanie handed Mrs. Mead the note.

I saw Jenny Carlin grinning at Angela Kemp.

Mrs. Mead must have read the note through at least three times while we stood there in front of the class. Finally she looked up at us and said, "All right, girls — please take your seats."

It was so quiet that we sounded like elephants clomping across the room. Mrs. Mead waited until we'd gotten completely settled before she went back to talking about the solar system.

I certainly didn't feel any better, though, because every minute that passed was a minute closer to Mrs. Wainwright's office. I'm usually starving by the time the bell rings for lunch, but not that day. Not even macaroni and cheese could calm my stomach down, especially with only about five seconds to eat. Besides, lots of kids stopped by our table to ask us questions.

"So, what happened? You had a sleepover last night and overslept?" Mark Freedman dropped down on the chair next to Patti's.

"No, they took one look at the school this morning and decided to keep on riding," Henry Larkin said with a grin. He must have seen us whiz past.

"Your biggest mistake was coming back," said Steven Gitten, who sat down next to Stephanie. It looked as though Jenny Carlin was going to fall off her chair three tables away, but I was too nervous to enjoy it.

The cafeteria is just across the hall from Mrs. Wainwright's office. At twelve-thirteen, Kate sighed loudly and said, "Let's get this over with."

"Good luck," said Steven Gitten.

"It's not *that* bad," Henry Larkin added. He'd been in the principal's office a couple of times.

Kate, Patti, Stephanie, and I trudged through Mrs. Jamison's office and into Mrs. Wainwright's.

There's a long, cream-colored couch on the side of the room opposite her desk, but we didn't get to sit on the couch. Four metal folding chairs were lined up right in front of Mrs. Wainwright, one for each of the Sleepover Prisoners.

"Please sit down," Mrs. Wainwright said. "And no talking." I couldn't have talked if I'd wanted to, my mouth was so dry!

We quietly sat there, while Mrs. Wainwright wrote on a yellow pad, looked at her appointment book, and walked back and forth to consult with Mrs. Jamison.

Mrs. Wainwright didn't even glance at us, and we certainly didn't look at her. Kate gazed at the wall, Patti looked down at her sneakers, Stephanie stared straight ahead without blinking — she was probably worrying about her dad.

Behind us, in the hall, some kids were whispering and giggling. One of them sounded a lot like Jenny Carlin, but I wasn't about to turn around to find out. I sat so stiffly that my neck started to ache.

I counted to a thousand. I went through the multiplication tables twice. I tried to think of all the foreign words I know — they're mostly about food, like teriyaki and burritos.

Thank goodness a baseball game started up outside on the playground — it gave me something to think about. Every minute or two, I could hear yelling:

One boy: "Strike three!"

Second boy: "Get real! That was high and outside!"

Third boy: "Larry, you're *out*! Batter up!"

Second boy: "Larkin, you need glasses!"

I tried to guess who was pitching, and who was catching, and formed a picture in my mind of Larry Jackson's face turning red, the way it does when he gets mad.

But those thirty-five minutes were still the longest thirty-five minutes of my life!

When the bell for afternoon classes finally rang, Mrs. Wainwright said, "I want each of you to write a full page for me, by tomorrow, about why it's not a good idea to be late to school . . . *aside* from the fact that you have to spend lunch hour in the principal's office." She absolutely read my mind! "That's it — get back to your room."

"Thank you, Mrs. Wainwright." We stood up and bolted through the door.

"After that, three minutes and ten seconds at Amateur Night will be a piece of cake," Kate whispered, and I agreed with her.

Chapter
7

That week we didn't have any time to practice our routine for Amateur Night. We were much too busy.

On Monday afternoon, we all had to write our papers for Mrs. Wainwright, about what being late means. I basically said it wasn't a good idea to be late because you might miss out on learning something really important at school, something that could change your life.

Then, on Tuesday afternoon, while Stephanie and Kate were getting stuff together for the yard sale — we'd decided to have it on Saturday morning, and Kate's parents had said okay — Patti came over to my house to help me look through Mom's magazine collection and snip out the entry blanks.

As I've mentioned, I'm definitely on the messy side. I think I inherited it from my mom. The only difference is that I spread my messiness around, and she keeps hers hidden in the basement.

There are mountains of cardboard boxes in our basement, full of things Mom can't bring herself to get rid of, like notebooks from her college days, or bunches of dried-up flowers from dances my father took her to when they were dating, or shoes that went out of style before I was born. Besides that, there are piles of old newspapers and magazines that she says she wants to look through again before she throws them out.

We armed ourselves for our trip to the basement with my desk lamp and Roger's, since the overhead light wasn't working, two pairs of scissors, a bag of chocolate-chip cookies, and two bottles of Cherry Coke. Rocky came with us — Rocky's my kitten, a brother of Patti's Adelaide, Kate's Fredericka, and Stephanie's Cinders.

Rocky curled up on a cardboard box and went to sleep. I sat down next to one stack of magazines, Patti next to another.

"Check the final day the entries can be received," I told her, "just to make sure the contests aren't already over."

Then we started flipping pages and clipping. "Here's a good one," Patti said. " 'Win! Enter now! Over 1,200 prizes! Grand prize: four-day trip for two to San Francisco, with luxury hotel accommodations, meals at world-famous restaurants . . . or *fifteen-hundred dollars in cash*!' Even the one hundred third-prize winners end up with thirty-inch color TVs."

"What's the date?" I asked.

"Um . . . about two weeks from now," Patti said.

"Cut it out and stick it under your lamp," I directed.

Not only did we go through all the women's magazines we could find (I ran across a great recipe for strawberry ice-cream pie with a chocolate cookie crust), we went through Dad's natural history magazines — "Win an exciting trip to the Amazon!" — and Roger's car magazines — "Win a fun-filled weekend to the Indianapolis Speedway!"

We flipped and clipped for a couple of hours, until my mom opened the basement door. "Patti, your mother called. She'll be here to pick you up in a few minutes."

"Coming!" I said.

Patti put her scissors down. "Wow," she said, picking up her stack of entry blanks. "There must be

57

about fifty here, and you've got even more. We still have to fill them all out."

She was right. We'd both forgotten about that. There were hours of work left.

"I'm sorry to leave you with all this," Patti apologized. "But Dad's giving a lecture tonight, so my mom and Horace" — he's Patti's little brother — "and I are going out for dinner."

"That's okay," I said. "My handwriting can use a little practice." It was true. Kate's father had once joked that I should think about being a doctor, since I already had the right handwriting to scribble prescriptions. "I'll fill them out tonight and ask Dad to mail them for me at the post office tomorrow."

"Sorry," Patti said again. "See you in the morning."

When we climbed the stairs, Mom glanced at the stack of little squares of paper I held and asked, "What were you girls doing down there, anyway?"

"Oh, just looking through your old magazines," I answered. I couldn't tell her about Stephanie's family problems. We'd all decided we'd be kind of vague with our parents about the yard sale, too, just telling them it was for a "good cause."

Meanwhile, Kate and Stephanie had been working away over at Stephanie's house. As Kate put it,

"Your basement is too much of a horror show for me, Lauren." She's so neat that she'd probably have to clean up the whole place before she'd feel comfortable enough to open a single magazine. So Kate was helping Stephanie sort through the clothes hanging in her closet and jammed into her chest-of-drawers, and pulling out things to sell at the yard sale.

I saw the stuff the next afternoon, when Patti, Kate, and I rode our bikes over. We were going to start sneaking it out of the Greens' house and into Kate's garage.

I couldn't believe what Stephanie had decided to sell! Her newest red sweatshirt with the big black squares; her red-and-white striped turtleneck sweater from a boutique in the city . . . and the black leather jacket, the one I was supposed to be wearing for calling Jenny Carlin on the phone!

"You're selling your jacket?" I exclaimed.

Stephanie nodded. "And my black western belt, and my beaded moccasins, and my red leather pocketbook, and — "

"How much do you want for the jacket?" I asked in spite of myself. I mean, I was terribly sorry about the money problems they were having, and I didn't want to be taking advantage. On the other hand, why should a total stranger end up with the jacket, or, even worse, somebody like Jenny or Angela?

Stephanie seemed to feel the same way. "Well, I've worn it a lot . . . I guess twenty dollars would be fair," she said. "Why don't you buy it, Lauren? At least that way it'll stay in the family."

I just happened to have gotten fifteen dollars in a letter from my grandmother, and I was pretty sure I could get an advance on my allowance from my dad for the extra five dollars.

"I'll take it!" I said. I put it on, and it fit perfectly — what Stephanie had taken up in width, I took up in length.

Patti said she'd buy the belt, which has a silver buckle with a blue stone in the center, for nine dollars. Kate picked out a black-and-white sweatshirt that looked great with her blonde hair — seven dollars.

"I've made . . . thirty-six dollars already," Stephanie said brightly. She was being a lot braver about having to sell her things than I would've been.

We filled up four backpacks and Stephanie's canvas tote with clothes. Then Stephanie opened her bedroom door. "Come on," she whispered, tiptoeing down the hall.

As we got closer to the kitchen, we could hear Mrs. Green on the telephone. "Yes," she was saying, "I know, Mother. It's going to take some juggling.

But we have to do *some*thing about the house. We just can't . . . okay. Yes, I'll call you later." She hung up.

Stephanie looked around at us. " 'Afford it.' I know she was going to say 'afford it,' " she murmured.

"Stephanie, is that you?" Mrs. Green called from the kitchen. "Hello, Kate . . . Lauren . . . Patti — I didn't know you were here. What are the Sleepover Friends up to now?" she added with a smile.

What *were* we up to?

"We're just going over to Kate's for a while, Mom," Stephanie said quickly.

"You look pretty loaded down," Mrs. Green said, checking out our backpacks. I don't think she noticed I was wearing the leather jacket, though.

Mrs. Green ruffled Stephanie's curly hair. "All right — don't forget that Daddy's cooking dinner."

On our way up the street, Kate said to Stephanie, "I didn't know your dad cooked."

"He's been cooking a lot lately," Stephanie said gloomily. "He's got nothing else to do."

"I thought your mother seemed kind of cheerful," I told her.

"It's all an act," Stephanie said with a nod of her head. "She's acting cheerful for *my* benefit."

61

Chapter 8

We stored Stephanie's clothes in the closet in Kate's garage, which is neater than most people's living rooms.

"My dad's going to try to sell our old lawn mower and a shovel and some rakes," Kate said. "And I've already filled a shopping bag with clothes that I don't wear anymore, plus some stuff Melissa's outgrown. Whatever we can get for it will go into the Green fund."

Patti nodded. "I'll be bringing some jeans and things that I'm too tall for now, and Horace's ant farm — the ants all escaped, but the farm's in great shape."

"Roger's giving us a stack of his old albums," I

told them. "He said we could keep the money."

"Thanks, guys," Stephanie said, looking down at the ground and clearing her throat. "You're really being great."

"Hey, listen — we'd better get started on our posters," I said, trying to lighten things up. "Only four more days until the sale, and it pays to advertise."

Kate had a stack of cardboard she'd taken out of Dr. Beekman's shirts when they came back from the laundry, and we went to work on it with felt-tip pens and some stickers.

"What should we say?" Patti asked, taking the top off of a neon-green pen.

" 'Yard sale' in big letters at the top, with '7 Pine Street' right under that," Kate said.

Stephanie giggled for the first time that afternoon. "Maybe we should add, 'Next door to Donald Foster,' " she said. "All the girls in seventh grade would come, and the sixth-graders, too."

"It wouldn't hurt," I agreed. "Then, 'Saturday,' and the date and time. . . ."

"What time?" Stephanie asked.

"People like to go to yard sales early — let's make it nine o'clock," Kate replied.

"Then a list of what we're going to be selling," I said. "Like, clothing, lawn mower, gardening tools, record albums. . . ."

"Toys — there's a whole box of toys in our attic that Horace has stopped playing with," Patti remembered.

"Maybe shoes, too," I added. "I can't believe Mom needs to hang onto those shoes in our basement."

We made enough posters to take to Charlie's Soda Fountain and Dandelion, a great store for kids' clothes, both on Main Street; Tully's Fish Market, Just Juniors, Sweet Stuff, and the Pizza Palace at the mall, and a couple of other places, too. We stuck stars and rainbows all around the edges of the posters, to brighten them up. Then we started biking them around town.

Of course, once we'd taped our poster to the inside of the front window at Charlie's, we *had* to have some double-dip pistachio cones. Next we shared a bag of chocolate-covered almonds, Stephanie's favorites, at Sweet Stuff. Then we needed something to cut through all that sugar, or at least I did.

"Next stop for a poster — Pizza Palace," I said. "I wouldn't mind a slice of pepperoni pizza."

64

"Lauren, how could you?" Stephanie groaned. "I'm stuffed, and it's practically dinnertime."

"Look out, Rhode Island!" Kate said. She hadn't forgotten Melissa's map.

But I wasn't the only one who thought pizza would hit the spot. It just so happened that half the boys in 5B were inside the Pizza Palace, playing video games and chowing down.

Pizza Palace is about the farthest thing from a palace you could imagine. It's one tiny room, with four video games crammed shoulder to shoulder in front, then a long counter with stools, and a big pizza oven against the back wall.

The oven usually raises the temperature inside the Pizza Palace to about a hundred degrees. I couldn't tell if Larry Jackson's face was beet-red because he was roasting, or because he was mad at the Alien Attackers game he was playing.

Mark Freedman was practically glued to the Turkey Shoot screen, so he couldn't manage more than a "Hi." But Steven Gitten and Henry Larkin were sitting at the counter, waiting for their slices, and they spun around on their stools a few times when we walked in.

"Hey!" Henry said to us.

"Hey, Stephanie," said Steven. He'd moussed

65

his short hair, and it was standing up in light-brown spikes.

Kate walked to the back to talk to the pizza cook, who was just sliding a pie out of the oven on a wide wooden paddle. "Hello, John — would you mind if we put our poster up on your wall?"

"Let's have a look." John read it through, then nodded. "Sure — go ahead. Maybe I'll come myself. I could use a lawn mower."

"You're having a yard sale?" Henry said as we taped the poster to the wall next to announcements for a church bingo tournament and a comedy performance by the Riverhurst Players.

I nodded. "Saturday at nine o'clock, at Kate's house — stuff from all four of our families."

"Is there room for anybody else?" Steven asked.

"What do you mean?" Kate said.

"Anybody can come who wants to," I said.

"No — actually, I've got some junk I'd like to get rid of. For money," Steven replied.

"Yeah, so do I!" said Henry Larkin. "My old ice-skates, and two radio-control racers, just a little bashed up. They had a head-on collision. . . ."

". . . some drawing books and one of those video-art sets I've only used once." Mark had given up on Turkey Shoot. "My aunt thought I was going to be an artist. She was wrong," he added with a grin.

"What about a slightly weird electronic keyboard?" Larry said, still hunched over Alien Attackers.

"What's wrong with it?" Henry asked him.

"No matter what you punch, it plays the same tune over . . . and over . . . and — "

"Game's over!" the Alien Attackers game announced. It made a couple of rude whistles.

"Nuts!" muttered Larry, giving the machine a smack with his hand before he fed it another quarter.

"A slice, please," I said to John. "With pepperoni."

"Should we let 'em?" Kate asked, looking at Patti, Stephanie, and me.

Stephanie shrugged. "Why not? We're not trying to sell the same kinds of things. . . . You guys can be in the sale," she said to Steven.

"Great!" Steven and Mark said.

"Bring something to lay your stuff out on," Kate added. "We don't have any extra card tables."

"No problem — my mom has some," Henry said.

"We'll be at your house at eight-thirty to set up," Mark said.

"We're going to be rich!" said Henry.

That was only the beginning. By the end of the week, we'd added Donald Foster. . . .

"If you're using me to advertise, I ought to be getting something out of it, right?" Donald had seen the poster for the sale at Charlie's, and he cornered Kate and me on the sidewalk in front of Kate's. "I've got some stuff I'd like to unload. . . ."

"Fair is fair," Stephanie said when we called her about it. "Besides, Donald *is* kind of cute."

"All this worry has clouded her mind," Kate said to me.

And Melissa. . . .

"I'm going to sell my own stuff, whether you like it or not!" Melissa stuck her tongue out at her sister. "And so is Sandy Bach. Mom said we could, so there!"

"Who is Sandy Bach?" I asked Kate.

"Melissa's latest best friend," Kate said. "She seems like a quiet kid, but I'm sure she won't be by the time Melissa gets through with her."

And Tod Schwartz, who lives across the street from Stephanie. Tod's on the high school football team. He had mentioned to Roger that he wanted to sell some of his exercise equipment because he's gotten too strong for it, and Roger told him about the yard sale.

"It's not a yard sale anymore," Kate grumbled at the sleepover on Friday. "It's a flea market!"

We were in the den at my house, putting price tags on the things we hadn't marked already.

"What about the ant farm?" Patti asked. "It was a floor model and only cost ten ninety-five to begin with, and that included the ants."

"One-fifty," Stephanie said. "Maybe *more* sellers will bring *more* buyers," she added to Kate. Stephanie held up a red-and-black skirt, looking at the front and back to see what kind of shape it was in. Then she wrote "$5.50" on a piece of tape, and stuck the tape to the skirt. "I hope so, anyway," she said with a sigh. "Today my dad didn't even bother to *pretend* he was still working. When I got home from school, he was sitting in the living room in a *T-shirt and jeans*, reading the newspaper."

"Maybe he was reading the job section," Patti suggested.

Stephanie shook her head. "Sports."

Kate stood up. "Does anybody want more pie?" I'd used the recipe I'd found in the basement to make the strawberry ice-cream chocolate-cookie pie, and it was yummy.

"Not yet — I'm on taco chips and bean dip for now," I said, digging into an economy-size bag of chips.

"No, thanks," Patti said.

"Why not?" Stephanie sighed. She was too down to even get excited about dieting.

"I'll bring you a piece." Kate had barely gotten to the kitchen, though, when she shouted, "I'll kill her!"

Stephanie, Patti, and I dropped everything and raced in there.

"Kill who?" I asked, since the kitchen was completely empty of people or animals. Rocky was back in the den, asleep, and Bullwinkle, my brother's big, black, part Newfoundland, was locked in the spare room upstairs. Besides, they're both boys.

"Look at my bedroom window!" Kate said through gritted teeth, pointing out the back door.

Kate's bedroom is upstairs and at the back of the Beekmans' house. You can see her window perfectly from my kitchen. Even though the Fosters' house is between us, it doesn't get in the way because it's set a little closer to the street.

Patti, Stephanie, and I peered out the back door.

"Your light's on?" Patti said.

"Right!" Kate was fuming. "And since *I* turned it off, *who* turned it on?"

"Your mom," Stephanie suggested.

"No way — she and Dad were going to bed early. He was worn out from being at the hospital last night, and she's tired from neatening up the yard for the sale tomorrow."

"Melissa's the only one left," I said.

"Melissa and Sandy Bach!" said Kate grimly. "She's sleeping over tonight, and I'll bet you the two of them are messing around in my room. Sisters! You don't know how lucky you are, Stephanie, to be an only child."

Stephanie nodded. "I don't think we could afford two, anyway."

Chapter
9

The yard sale started slowly the next morning, but by ten o'clock, the place was really jumping.

Donald's table was surrounded with girls, fighting to buy his used tapes and worn-out sweatshirts. The guys from 5B were doing a big business with seven- and eight-year-old boys, unloading their bashed racers, slightly weird electronic keyboards, and old skates. Henry Larkin was counting dollar bills, Steven Gitten was grinning from ear to ear, and Larry's face was a nice, calm color for a change. Even Melissa and Sandy Bach had buyers at their table, which was covered with ratty-looking stuffed animals, and a collection of dolls with matted hair. The girls looked smug every time they saw us. Kate was saving her talk with Melissa until later.

Our three tables were farther down the lawn, between Tod Schwartz's exercise equipment and Dr. Beekman's yard tools — John from Pizza Palace actually came to buy the lawn mower!

"It pays to advertise," I said wisely.

Our clothes were selling like hotcakes, especially Stephanie's. Some of her stuff would fit older girls, too, so besides having a lot of fifth-grade customers — Robin Becker and Jane Sykes from our class and Betsy Chalfin from 5C and Tracy Osner from 5A — and their mothers, we were doing great with the overflow from Donald Foster.

My mom slept late that Saturday, and Mrs. Beekman was busy inside the house. By the time they wandered outside to take a look around, the Sleepover Friends had already made almost one hundred dollars for the Green fund.

"My goodness!" Mrs. Beekman said when she saw the pile of money. "What are you girls selling?"

"Oh, just some toys, albums, and . . . clothes," Kate replied briskly, with a warning glance at us.

My mother took a closer look at the things stacked on our tables. "Why, Barbara!" she murmured to Mrs. Beekman. "Some of these things have never been worn!"

"Uh-oh," Kate muttered.

73

Mom held up a brand-new red-and-black sweater. "Who does this belong to?"

"Oh. It's mine, Mrs. Hunter," Stephanie answered. "I decided it didn't go with the rest of my stuff." A pretty lame excuse, since almost all of her clothes are red, black, and white.

"And these?" Mrs. Beekman picked up a pair of black jeans with the tags still on them.

"They're . . . uh . . . mine, too," Stephanie replied uncomfortably.

"Does your mother know you're selling new clothes?" Mrs. Beekman asked Stephanie.

"Well, of *course* she does, Mom!" Kate interrupted.

Mrs. Beekman raised an eyebrow at her daughter. "Ann," she said to my mother, "won't you join me inside for a cup of coffee?"

"Lovely," my mother said.

The two of them headed across the lawn and up the front steps of the Beekmans' house. Their heads were together, and they were talking a mile a minute. They looked back at us before they stepped through the door.

"Oh, dear . . . ," Patti said.

"They'll start drinking coffee and forget about it," Kate predicted. "Everything will be fine."

"It has to be," said Stephanie, taking five dollars from a redheaded fourth-grader for the jeans.

My mom and Mrs. Beekman stayed inside. Not ten minutes had passed, however, when a car pulled up on the opposite side of Pine Street — our side was jammed with the parked cars of shoppers.

"Stephanie, it's your mother!" Kate hissed.

By the time Mrs. Green had gotten out of her car and crossed the street, my mom and Mrs. Beekman were waiting for her at the curb. They marched up the lawn side by side, toward us.

"Stephanie, I hope you have some kind of explanation as to why you're selling most of your clothes," Mrs. Green said when she got to our table. I'd never seen her look angry before — not even annoyed.

"I'm not selling *most* . . . ," Stephanie began, but Mrs. Green held up a hand to stop her. "I have looked through your closet, young lady, and at least half of your hangers are empty! Some of your favorite things are gone — your western belt, the black leather jacket. . . ." Mrs. Green stopped. She had finally spotted it on me.

"Mom, I had to," Stephanie said. Her lower lip started to tremble.

"Why did you have to? If you needed money

75

for something, Daddy would have — "

Didn't Mrs. Green know about the loan? Anyway, that's the very next thing Stephanie blurted out. "We saw Daddy at the bank, borrowing money!"

"Since he's not working now, we decided to help out by — " Kate stuck in.

"Oh, my heavens," Mrs. Green exclaimed. I couldn't believe it, but she was starting to smile. "You saw Stephanie's father taking out a loan at the bank, and you came to the conclusion that he'd lost his job. . . ."

"Hasn't he? The two of you have been acting so strange," Stephanie said. "Whispering, worrying about the house, not telling me what's going on, and Daddy sitting around the living room on a weekday in his jeans and T-shirt!"

"Well," said Mrs. Green, "Daddy has *not* lost his job. In fact, Mr. Binder just gave him a raise. And I have an announcement to make. I was saving it until dinner tonight. . . ." She looked at Patti, Kate, and me. "But if you all aren't family, I don't know who is." Mrs. Green put her arm around Stephanie. "Honey . . . we're going to have a baby!"

"Oh, a baby!" my mom and Mrs. Beekman squealed together.

"A baby . . . ," Stephanie said softly.

Chapter 10

As Mrs. Green explained, Mr. Green had stayed home on Friday to take her to the doctor. "We wanted to be certain that everything was okay before we discussed it with you, sweetie," she said to Stephanie.

And the loan was for an addition to their house. "The baby will have a room to him- or herself," Mrs. Green went on. "Next to our bedroom, and far enough away from your room so that you won't be disturbed by the crying. Or the baby by sleepover goings-on," she added with a smile.

"A baby . . . ," Stephanie repeated for the third or fourth time.

She's always been an only child — it's going to take some getting used to.

Mrs. Green and Mrs. Beekman and my mom left to check out the crowd for Stephanie's clothes — they'd already grabbed my black leather jacket.

We'd sold most of Patti's, Kate's, and my stuff when Kate suddenly yelled, "Today's my lucky day! Look — there's my dad's fishing hat!"

It was squashed onto the head of a man wearing green overalls that said, "Pete — Bennett Oil" over the pocket. For two pairs of our jeans (for Pete's daughter) and a rusty rake from Dr. Beekman, we got the hat back, more or less in one piece.

Besides the fishing hat, we ended up with one hundred and two dollars and thirty-eight cents, even after Stephanie had bought back most of her clothes.

"That's a lot of money. What are we going to do with it?" I asked.

"I know we don't need it for the Green fund anymore, but it doesn't seem right, somehow, to just spend it on ourselves," Patti said.

Kate spoke up. "We don't *have* to spend it on ourselves. What if we give it to some babies who really need it — like the ones at the Riverhurst Children's Hospital? My mom's on the fund-raising committee, and they're having a drive right now to make money for the Infant Care Unit."

"Sounds perfect!" Patti said.

"Excellent!" I echoed. Stephanie just grinned.

"I'll ask Mom how to do it," said Kate.

The crowd had thinned out, so everybody started cleaning up the lawn and getting ready to leave. The boys from 5B helped us pack up what was left of our stuff and carry it into the garage.

"Who knows?" said Kate. "Maybe we'll do this again."

"You bet!" Henry Larkin said. "I made thirty-six dollars — I think I'll use part of it to add a couple of tricks to our magic act for Friday."

Friday! In all the excitement, I'd managed to forget totally about Amateur Night. And I was afraid Stephanie wasn't going to be that much help for a while. She was already busy thinking up names. "Vanessa," she said as we stacked our leftover clothes on a shelf in the garage closet. "No. Kimberly . . . or Clarissa. And maybe a cute little red-and-white bedroom, with black-and-white tiles."

"It might not be a girl," I pointed out.

"And if it is, she could grow up to be just like Melissa," warned Kate.

Stephanie looked thoughtful. "Alexander," she said at last. "Jeremy. Brian."

"With little boys, you're likely to end up with a

houseful of creepy crawlies," Patti reminded her. Patti's little brother, Horace, collects snakes, lizards, frogs, turtles — all the slimers.

"Not if I train the kid from an early age to do as I tell him," Stephanie said breezily.

Kate, Patti, and I looked at each other and shrugged our shoulders. Did she ever have a lot to learn!

We did get in a couple of hours of practice on our routine on Sunday afternoon, on Tuesday after school, and a little on Thursday. But I can't exactly say I was ready. I would never really be ready to go onstage and make a fool of myself in front of hundreds of people!

Stephanie's dad drove us to the auditorium that Friday night. We got there around seven. We were wearing denim minis, tights, crop-tops, and lots of bangles, and we'd pulled the top of our hair over in side ponytails, just like the Polka Dots.

The show wouldn't be starting until seven-thirty, but we wanted to see where we were in the line-up. I was also hoping my stomach would settle down in the thirty minutes before curtain time.

Backstage, some of the kids were warming up.

Karla Stamos was twirling around on her toes in a brown leotard and tutu. Angela was in the corner with Jenny, who was squawking away on her clarinet.

Henry Larkin and Larry Jackson were running through some of their magic act: pulling scarves out of thin air, making paper flowers disappear, and ending up with a trick where Larry takes his little sister's rabbit out of a supposedly empty hat.

They were good — everybody clapped except Jenny Carlin. Maybe she was in a bad mood because her clarinet sounded so awful, and maybe she was afraid nobody would clap for her. But that's no excuse for what she did next. "You can tell that rabbit comes from Larry's family," she whispered to Angela. "There's something familiar about those ears."

Larry's ears do stick out, but so what? His face turned a dark red, and it wasn't because he was warm.

Before he could say anything, though, Mr. Coulter handed us some programs — he's the music teacher at Riverhurst Elementary, and he handles all of the stage performances. "Hot off the presses," he said. The Four Aces were near the end, between Karen Sims, a girl from 5A who sings really well, and Steven Gitten's juggling act.

My stomach was still hopping around when the lights blinked on and off. "Five minutes to show-time!" Mr. Coulter called out.

Chairs scraped in the auditorium on the other side of the curtain, the uproar quieted — the audience was waiting. Karla, who was the first performer, handed her tape to Mr. Coulter.

The curtain rose slowly, the tape clicked on, and as classical music poured out of the big speakers, Karla swept onto the stage. She wasn't bad, really — we were watching from the wings. She did some jumps that were kind of neat. It's just that the music went on for so long!

"It's like being in a marathon!" Kate murmured. "I'd die! I'd absolutely die!"

"Ours is only three minutes and ten seconds," Stephanie said soothingly. "Do you guys like the name Karla?"

When Karla was finally finished, Tommy Brown from 5C played a short tune on his trumpet, Robin Becker played ragtime on the piano, and Henry and Larry did their magic act. They got lots of applause.

Two girls from 5A played violins together. "The violin is really difficult," Patti whispered. She's probably right, but they definitely needed some practice.

Then it was Jenny's turn. She walked onto the

82

stage, smiled sweetly, put the end of her clarinet in her mouth, blew . . . and nothing happened. Jenny frowned. She blew harder . . . nothing!

Larry and Henry were huddled behind a cardboard tree backstage, their hands over their mouths, practically gagging with laughter. It must have been contagious, because the four of us started giggling, too.

Jenny wiggled her fingers up and down the keys . . . blew . . . silence. She shook the clarinet . . . tried again . . . nothing. Even the audience was beginning to titter.

Jenny gave it one more try. She twisted the bottom piece of the clarinet a little, stuck the top back in her mouth, and with the most determined look I'd ever seen, she blew.

There was a hideous squawk, and something like a real note came out. Jenny honked along like that for a few more notes, that grim look still on her face. Then a kid in the front row gestured frantically. When he saw that he had her attention, he motioned for her to turn the clarinet upside down. Jenny stuck two fingers inside the clarinet . . . and pulled out the end of a blue silk scarf!

I recognized it — it was one of the scarves from Henry and Larry's magic act. Jenny looked up just then and saw us standing in the wings — Henry and Larry had disappeared.

"We had nothing to do with it!" Stephanie mouthed, guessing what Jenny was thinking.

But Jenny didn't look convinced. For the moment, though, she had other things to attend to. She tossed the scarf to one side, took a deep breath, and picked up her solo where she'd left off. I had to hand it to her — that was brave.

She got through it with nothing more embarrassing than a couple of squeaks. As the audience clapped (with relief, I thought), she marched off the stage. Before any of us could say a word, she hissed, "Not very smart of you!" and stalked away.

"She's going to try to get us," I predicted.

"What can she do here?" said Kate.

Another ten minutes, and we were on. We'd already given our tape to Mr. Coulter, so we ran out onstage the way rock-and-rollers do, lined up, and waited for the opening chorus of "I Wanna Be Your Girl." Instead, we got violins and French horns!

Stephanie, Patti, Kate, and I stared at each other.

"What's happening?" Stephanie whispered.

"Jenny Carlin!" I groaned, nodding toward the wings. Jenny and Angela were smirking at us. Somehow, they'd managed to switch our tape with Karla's!

84

Chapter
11

"What should we do?" Patti whispered, panic-stricken.

I was ready to beat a fast retreat, myself.

"We'll just do our routine," Stephanie muttered. "Follow my lead."

Kate, Patti, and I followed as Stephanie picked up the beat and started to go through our act, spreading her arms out wide, hopping forward on one foot, hopping back, doing the moonwalk, and all the other steps we'd worked out for "I Wanna Be Your Girl."

The audience went bananas. They thought we'd planned the whole thing as a joke. There was just one problem — Mr. Coulter thought we had, too. After he'd slipped the cassette into the machine, he walked away to check on the next performers. And we couldn't possibly keep this up for as long as Karla had!

Good old Larry Jackson and Henry Larkin came to our rescue. After about four minutes of us bouncing around onstage, they pulled the tape out. We bowed, and the audience applauded so loudly it sounded like thunder. Thanks to Jenny, we were the stars of Amateur Night!

"And the stars deserve a celebratory meal!" Mr. Green said when it was all over. The sleepover was at Stephanie's house that night, so her parents drove the four of us to Mimi's, an Italian restaurant near the university.

It's true, I made a pig of myself. I ate stuffed clams, salad, pizza with everything except anchovies, and a butterscotch sundae.

I don't know whether it was the excitement of Amateur Night or all that food. But when we finally got to sleep, I had really odd dreams about Steven Gitten juggling Larry Jackson's rabbit, the Greens' new baby doing a tap dance, and Jenny Carlin making the most awful sounds on a huge clarinet.

That's probably why, when I first heard the strange noise the next morning, I thought I was still dreaming. I covered up my head and kept dozing. Kate, Stephanie, and Patti didn't open their eyes, either, until Mrs. Green rushed into Stephanie's bedroom.

"Stephanie, wake up!" she said sharply.

"What is it?" Stephanie said, yawning.

"Have you entered any contests recently?" her mother asked.

"No, Mom," Stephanie answered, forgetting about all of those entry blanks I'd mailed in for her.

"Yes, we did," I said. "Did we actually win something?" I added eagerly.

"I guess you could say that," Mrs. Green replied.

And there was the horrible noise again, sort of a cross between a giant wheeze and a horn honking!

"What was *that*?" Kate sat straight up in bed, suddenly wide awake.

"That, girls, is your prize," Stephanie's mother said.

We didn't bother to change. We pulled sweatshirts on over our pajamas and raced outside. A large truck, with a ramp leading down to the street, was parked in front of the Greens' house. At the end of the ramp were Mr. Green, the truck driver . . . and a donkey! When it saw us, it opened its mouth and brayed loudly for the third time.

"Lauren seems to know something about this," Mrs. Green said to her husband.

The truck driver grinned as he handed the donkey's halter rope to Mr. Green. "You also get two free bales of hay," the man said, disappearing inside the truck.

The donkey had other ideas, though. He reached over and snipped the tops off several of Mrs. Green's petunias.

He was darling! Grayish-brown, with long ears and big brown eyes, he didn't look much bigger than Bullwinkle.

"He's gorgeous!" Stephanie said, patting his neck. "We're keeping him, right?"

"Stephanie, we can't possibly . . . ," her mother began.

"If he goes back, he's dog meat," said the truck driver, heaving a bale of hay onto the sidewalk.

"What is that supposed to mean?" Mr. Green said.

"I read an article about this once," Patti said — she never forgets anything she reads. "The government has started killing wild donkeys because there are so many on government lands out west. Then they send them to dog food factories. But they don't kill the ones who're adopted."

"That's right," said the truck driver. "A bunch of people called Friends of the Burro try to place them with families who'll take care of them."

I was trying to think. Had I really filled out an entry blank that said "Friends of the Burro"? I'd been so tired that night that it's possible I didn't read every shred of paper I wrote Stephanie's name on.

"Of course we'll take care of him!" Stephanie was saying.

"What are we going to do with a burro?" her father groaned.

"The baby will love him," Stephanie said cagily.

"And we can use him in our party business," Kate added. "He'll pay for himself."

"He already owes me six petunias," Mrs. Green said as the burro snipped off more flowers. "He *is* cute, though."

Mr. Green threw up his hands. "All right, all right," he said. "We'll keep him until I can find a better place for him. Maybe a petting zoo will take him. In the meantime, we'll build him a room, too," he joked. "I'll take out another loan."

"No more loans," said Mrs. Green. "I have a feeling that's how all of this got started."

"I think we'll call him Sleepover," Stephanie said. And, no kidding, the donkey bobbed his head up and down.

SLEEPOVER FRIENDS

#12 Kate's Sleepover Disaster

"I invited Wanda Barnes to the sleepover to-night, too," Rebecca Newman said.

Rebecca's cousin Reggie turned to Kate and asked, "You're staying at the Barnses', aren't you?"

"Yes," Kate answered.

Reggie grinned. "Keep your eye on Will — he's *something*."

"Who's Will?" I asked.

"The eight-year-old — he's my brother's age, and is he wild!" Reggie answered.

"Oh, great!" Kate groaned.

"Of course, the twins aren't exactly relaxing, either," Reggie went on. "And then there's Frank — the best wrestler at Walden High."

"Sounds perfect," said Kate. "I'm spending a week with three monsters and the Incredible Hulk."

WIN GIRL TALK—
A BRAND NEW TRUTH OR DARE GAME!

Enter the Great
SLEEPOVER
FRIENDS
CONTEST

100 Winners!

YOU can win a copy of the BRAND NEW game—Girl Talk! Play this exciting truth or dare game (by Golden) with your friends and have your own great sleepover party! All you have to do is enter the Great Sleepover Friends Contest. Complete the coupon below and return by May 31, 1989.

Playing games is not all Kate, Lauren, Stephanie and Patti do at their great sleepover parties! Truth or Dare, scary movies, late-night boy talk—it's all a part of **Sleepover Friends!**

- -

Sleepover Friends Girl Talk Contest

Where did you buy this book?

☐ Bookstore ☐ Drug Store ☐ Supermarket ☐ Other _____
☐ Discount Store ☐ Book Club ☐ Book Fair specify _____

Name _____

Birthday _____ Age _____

Street _____

City, State, Zip _____

SLE988